Along the RIVER NILE

Dear Reader

Imagine if you could transport yourself to the source of the Nile River right now! To travel the entire length of the river, you would have to stop in Uganda, at the Murchison Falls. There you'd meet Jamie and his team who operate Kayak the Nile. On pages 28–29 of this book, you can see some great action shots of Jamie kayaking the Nile.

> IT'S HARD NOT TO BE HAPPY ON SUCH AN AMAZING RIVER. ”
>
> JAMIE SIMPSON

Stop over in the Sudan, and you might also get the opportunity to observe the Nile Swimmers Project in action. It's an inspirational drowning-prevention program founded by two British lifesaving instructors. They train many people who live along the Nile, such as the Sudanese Sea Scouts, in water safety. Check out their story in Chapter 11, and enjoy your journey along the Nile.

Sharon Parsons

My sincere thanks to the following people for their time, information, images and enthusiasm for this book:

Tom Mecrow and Dan Graham, The Nile Swimmers Project, UK

Jamie Simpson, Kayak the Nile, Uganda

For learning solutions, visit **cengage.com.au**

Contents

Along the RIVER NILE

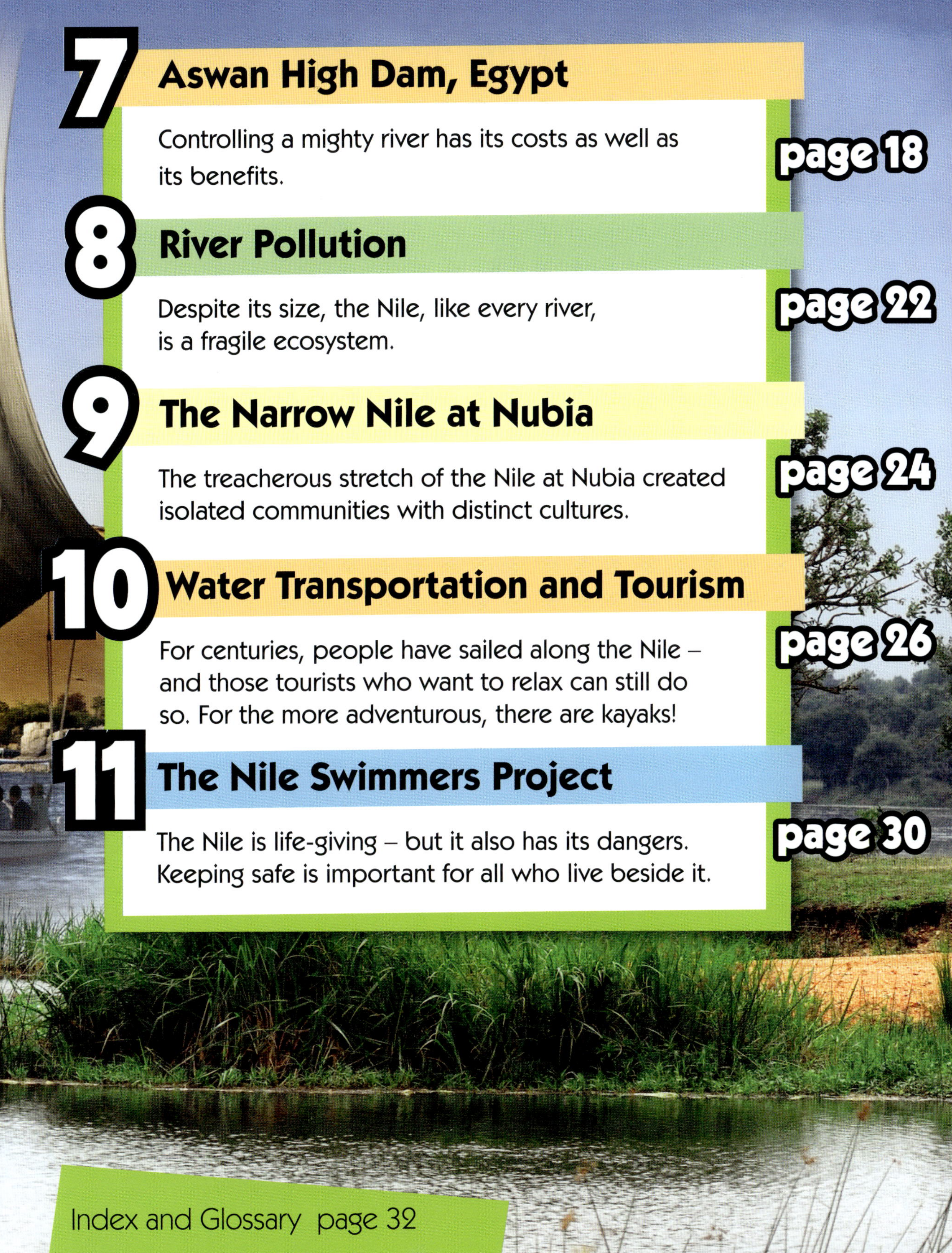

1 Introducing the Nile River

The Nile has offered a life-sustaining environment for some of the world's oldest civilisations, and continues to do so for the 160 million people who rely upon it today. For those who learned to understand its features and seasonal changes, the Nile has been central not only to survival, but to the evolution of cultures, the development of agriculture and the flourishing of great civilisations, such as the ancient Egyptian kingdoms.

NILE MEANING

The Nile's name is derived from the Greek word *Neilos*, which means river valley.

For around 6 650 kilometres, the mighty Nile and its tributaries flow through 11 countries in northeast and central-east Africa – a vast region known as the Nile Basin. Today, as it has done for thousands of years, the impact of the Nile Basin's unpredictable rainfall and diverse climate zones continues to affect the rise and fall of the Nile River's water levels.

The Nile River's journey through eleven countries in Africa, from the south to the Mediteranean Sea in the north.

River Lengths

- The Nile, Africa – 6 650 km
- The Amazon, South America – 6 570 km
- The Yangtze, China – 6 300 km
- The Murray, Australia – 2 600 km
- The Waikato, New Zealand – 435 km

Demands on the Nile's Resources

In the past, people living along the Nile had to adapt to its seasonal variations. Today, however, careful management of this life-giving resource is helping to give stability to the growing population that depends on it.

Living in a region with limited fertile land and unpredictable rainfall makes water management critical. This, combined with the fact that so many different countries are reliant on the Nile River, means that governments and water experts must continually try to resolve conflict and inequality arising over use of this precious water resource. Every country has increasing demands for a greater share of the Nile River's water: to build more irrigation canals for crops (less than 10 per cent of the land that could be irrigated currently is), to build dams for water storage (for low-rainfall times of the year) and to generate electricity (only 15 per cent of people living in the Nile Basin have access to electricity).

The Nile: Longest River in the World

Depending on how it is measured, from its source in central Africa until it meets the Mediterranean Sea, there are varying estimates of the Nile's length. The most commonly accepted length is around 6 650 kilometres, which makes the Nile the world's longest river.

The Amazon: Second Longest River in the World

The Amazon in South America is 6 570 kilometres in length. The Amazon is the largest river in the world, by volume of water carried. On average, an incredible 219 million litres of water flows into the ocean from the Amazon every second. That's around 20 percent of all the fresh water flowing into the world's oceans.

The Yangtze: Third Longest River in the World

The Yangtze in China is 6 300 kilometres in length. The world's largest hydroelectric project (Three Gorges Dam, Hubei province) is on the Yangtze River.

The Murray: Longest River in Australia

The Murray in New South Wales and South Australia is 2 600 kilometres in length.

The Waikato: Longest River in New Zealand

The Waikato in the North Island is 435 kilometres in length.

2 The Nile Basin

The Nile Basin is the area that encompasses the Nile River (including its associated tributaries, lakes and waterways) as well as the agricultural lands bordering the river. The Nile Basin covers an area that is equal to about 10 per cent of Africa, and includes parts of eleven countries.

Nile Basin Initiative

In 1999, the governments of ten countries in the Nile Basin (all the Nile Basin countries except Eritrea) formed the Nile Basin Initiative. Its key objective is "to achieve sustainable socio-economic development through the equitable utilization of, and benefit from, the common Nile Basin water resources".

THE NILE DELTA

In the shape of a triangle, the Nile Delta is about 160 kilometres long and 240 kilometres wide at the coast, and has highly fertile agricultural land, where rice and other crops are grown. Along its coastline are lagoons, wetlands, lakes and sand dunes. Its total area is estimated to be about 25 000 square kilometres.

The Nile Delta Ecosystem

The Nile Delta is one of the world's most vital migration stopovers for millions of birds, such as white pelicans, white storks, black storks and European cranes.

a migrating stork

425 million People in 11 Nile Basin Countries

Population of Countries in the Nile Basin

There are 11 countries in the Nile Basin, with a total population of about 425 million. Of this population, over 160 million people are directly affected by and reliant on the Nile River. By 2050, the population of the region is expected to double.

Egypt: 83 million
Ethiopia: 82 million
Democratic Republic of the Congo: 68 million
Tanzania: 45 million
Kenya: 41 million
Sudan: 37 million
Uganda: 35 million
Rwanda: 11 million
South Sudan: 9 million
Burundi: 9 million
Eritrea: 5 million

On 9 July 2011, the Republic of South Sudan gained independence from the Republic of Sudan.

Eritrea is not an official member of the Nile Basin Initiative, but takes an interest in its management.

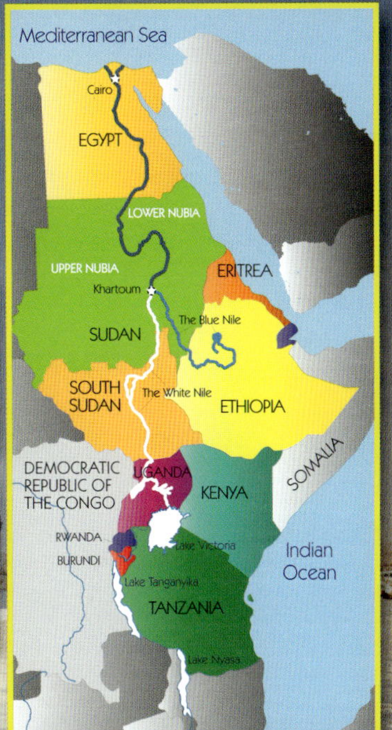

The Arab Republic of Egypt

Egypt is a desert-dominated country with minimal rainfall and less than four per cent of its total land suitable for growing crops. As a result, its reliance on the Nile River and the fertile land around it is absolute.

About 25 per cent of its working population are engaged in agricultural jobs and it is unlawful to build on land suitable for crops.

Egypt's capital city is Cairo, which has a population of nearly 20 million people.

In 1959 Egypt and Sudan made an agreement to share the Nile River's resources, with Egypt allocated 75% of the water and Sudan allocated 25%. That law is still in place and a source of ongoing discussion amongst other countries in the Nile Basin.

3 Journey Along the Nile River

The Nile River in Africa is the world's longest river, with a five-thousand-year history of human settlement and agricultural activity along its fertile banks. The civilisations that grew up along the Nile's long path included some of the world's earliest urban, literate societies, as well as many nomadic and village-based cultures. There are an array of agricultural, architectural and artistic traditions and techniques that have been practised by the peoples living along the Nile for thousands of years.

an aerial view of the Nile River today

One River, Many Countries

The Nile River and its tributaries flow through 11 different countries. The Nile is actually an intricate series of rivers, streams, waterfalls and rapids, combining to become a single mighty river. The main part of the Nile River begins in Uganda, flows through South Sudan and Sudan and finally reaches Egypt. There, the river flows past the famous pyramids, through the city of Cairo, and further north into the Nile Delta at the mouth of the river, where it joins the Mediterranean Sea.

the White Nile, Murchison Falls, Uganda

Diverse Environments and Wildlife

The Nile River winds its way through diverse and often impenetrable environments. It passes through a huge freshwater lake (Lake Victoria), tropical rainforests, bird-rich wetlands, grasslands, desert, hippo-filled marshes, swamps, mountains, plateaus and a river delta. As the Nile River winds its way northwards, it flows though increasingly expansive areas of desert in Sudan, until it finally reaches Egypt, which is about 96 per cent desert. Here, the Nile is the only plentiful source of fresh water.

A rich variety of plant and animal life has also made a home along the river's long and circuitous route northwards. Many animals, such as crocodiles and elephants, live in or beside the river year round, and others migrate with the seasons. Many migratory birds stop over in one of the world's largest wetlands, Al-Sudd (which means "the papyrus" in Arabic), in South Sudan.

Murchison Falls on the White Nile, Uganda

hippos in the Nile River at the Murchison Falls National Park, Uganda

an elephant on the shore of the Nile River in Uganda

The White Nile

There are three main streams that form the Nile River. In the south, Kagera River in Burundi flows into Lake Victoria, the second-largest freshwater lake in the world. Lake Victoria is so vast that it extends into three countries: Kenya, Uganda and Tanzania. The water then flows on from Lake Victoria in a number of streams that become the river known as the White Nile. Its name comes from the colour of its water, which is a cloudy grey due to particles from a whitish clay sediment.

The White Nile continues for about 800 kilometres. It flows through Lake Kyoga and Lake Albert, and on into South Sudan. There it is joined by the river Bahr al Ghazal. At that junction, the White Nile flows northwards through South Sudan's grasslands, tropical rainforests and swamps. There, the White Nile meets the Blue Nile.

NILE RIVER'S SOURCE

The furthest source of the Nile River has long been debated, but in recent times, Nile Basin authorities agree that the river's southernmost source is a headstream called the Ruvyironza in Burundi.

the White Nile in Uganda

The Blue Nile

The Blue Nile is the second of the three main streams that make up the Nile River. The Blue Nile begins in Ethiopia and flows down to join the White Nile at Khartoum in a semi-desert region of Sudan. Unlike the White Nile, the Blue Nile has a flood season, caused by summer monsoonal rains in Ethiopia. In high-rainfall years, monsoonal floods cause the Blue Nile to contribute almost 70 per cent of the Nile River's flow at Khartoum. Two dams in Sudan rely on good flows from the Blue Nile for water storage, irrigation and power supply for its people and oil production.

LOW RAINFALL YEARS

One example of successive low rainfall years occurred in the mid-1980s, when it led to extremely low water-storage levels in dams, such as the Aswan High Dam, Egypt. In 1988, higher rainfalls flowed throughout the Nile Basin and dam storage levels were restored.

fishing on the Blue Nile

The Blue Nile and the White Nile are the two river systems that contribute most of the flow of the Nile River. The two rivers meet at Khartoum, Sudan.

The Atbarah River

The Nile River (the combined White and Blue Niles) flows northeast from Khartoum for about 320 kilometres, when it meets the third main contributing stream, the Atbarah. Like the Blue Nile, the Atbarah River rises from the Ethiopian highlands. It then flows down into Sudan where it meets the Nile. The Atbarah River carries rich black sediment during high rainfall years, and like the Blue Nile it has a heavy flood season. It contributes more than 10 per cent of the total flow of the Nile, but almost all of that comes between July and October, during the summer floods.

THE WHITE NILE AND THE BLUE NILE

Both rivers have Arabic names (Arabic is the official language of many of the countries along the Nile River). The White Nile is called **Bahr al Abyad**, and the Blue Nile is called **Al-Bahr Al-Azraq**.

The Nile, a Life-Sustaining River

From the wide expanse of Lake Victoria to the vibrant birdlife of Al-Sudd in Sudan to the flood-swollen waters of the Blue Nile to the desert sands of Egypt, the Nile is as diverse as it is long. The only thing that remains constant is the river's importance to the countries it passes through. Managing the river's resources fairly and sustainably is the key challenge facing all of the countries of the Nile Basin.

4 The Nile River – a Food Source

To outside observers, it might seem that settling alongside a river that floods almost every year would not be a good idea. But this is exactly the reason that the great civilisations of ancient Egypt were able to thrive for thousands of years.

During the seasonal floods, vast quantities of fertile silt were brought from further south and deposited on the desert plains of Egypt. Once the floodwaters receded, huge areas of grain and other crops could be planted in the silt. Because the ancient Egyptians understood the seasonal changes, they could plan their entire agricultural system around the Nile. Every year, the Nile flooded and left behind an ideal environment for growing food. More food than could be eaten was grown, and the excess stored for the period until the floods came again, replenishing the soil with fresh silt and nutrients once more.

A Unique Ecosystem

Some years, the Nile did not flood, and the agricultural cycle was upset. Months or years of hardship might follow. But overall the Nile could be depended on to provide food and support agriculture, and it was this that enabled a great civilisation to establish itself in the middle of a desert.

Today, as the Nile flows northwards, it winds through unique ecosystems that provide millions of people with a life based on crops, fish and natural vegetation (e.g. papyrus reeds). The land along the Nile is very fertile but also very limited, so people plant crops intensively on the rich strip of soil by the river. Vegetables are grown at the base of citrus fruit trees and date palms to make the most of all arable land.

Papyrus

Papyrus reeds still grow in freshwater marshes along the Nile River, but its growth is controlled and therefore it is not as prevalent as it was in times past. Papyrus continues to be made into paper and packaging products. In ancient times papyrus was used to make a multitude of other things, such as furniture, mattresses, footwear, boats and rope. The papyrus root was used for medicine, food and perfume.

papyrus depicting ancient Egyptian history

papyrus plants growing on the Nile River

fishing on the Nile River

5 A Culinary Feast on the Nile

The people who live beside the Nile have always enjoyed the food from its fertile banks. There is evidence that in ancient times certain foods were only consumed by the rich, such as fish, meats and poultry, but the poor are known to have consumed geese, ducks and quails on special occasions. Some fish, meat and poultry was boiled or roasted and eaten immediately, but most was preserved in salt and left to dry in the sun.

An ancient Egyptian carving shows a person eating.

a quail

SALT FROM SIWA

Lake Siwa in Egypt is a very large saltwater lake. Today Siwa is famous for olives and dates, but the ancient Egyptians got their cooking salt from there.

A **Culture** Based on **Agriculture**

Bread by Hand, or Feet!

Bread was an important part of the ancient cultures along the Nile, and the tradition of eating flat breads of all kinds continues today. Ancient drawings show Egyptians mixing and kneading ingredients with their hands in bowls and also with their feet in larger tubs! Loaves of bread have been found in ancient Egyptian tombs, some in creative shapes such as the shape of a fish.

Baking Bread

The dough was placed in moulds, and baked in clay ovens or on open fires. Dough was also placed on clay disks and covered with a clay lid to create a mini-oven, and cooked over open fires, too.

An Egyptian farmer (below right) sorts grain for bread by hand.

a traditional clay oven

A Variety of Food

Some fruits and vegetables, as well as nuts, grains and pulses (beans, chickpeas, lentils and green peas) were an important part of the ancient Egyptian diet. They are still important to communities living in the Nile region today, and beyond its borders, too.

Fruits

Nuts

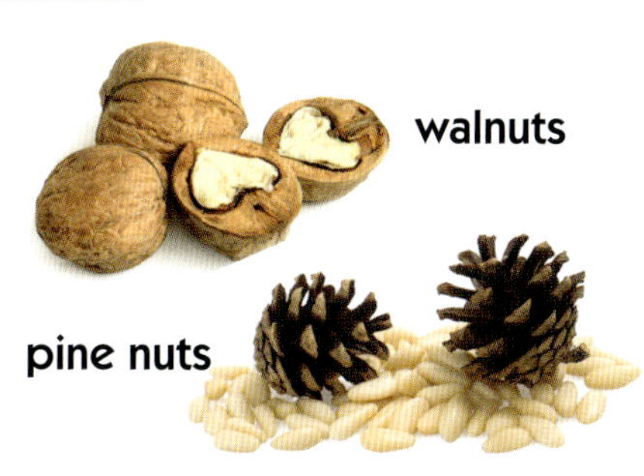

Flavoursome Foods

Foods were flavoured with spices such as cumin and mustard, and with strongly flavoured plants such as garlic, onions, coriander and wild radishes. Some foods, such as garlic and onions, were also used for medicinal purposes.

garlic

Cooking in Clay Ovens

Most foods were cooked in clay ovens, or in open fires, and plates were also made of clay. Food was baked, boiled, stewed, fried, grilled or roasted. But very little is known about how the food was prepared.

Eating Off Gold Plates!

Evidence shows that the wealthy ancient Egyptians ate from plates made of bronze, silver and gold, using the tips of their fingers to eat. After the meal they rinsed their fingers in small bowls of water on the table.

6 An Ancient Egyptian Recipe

Generally, there is little archaeological evidence of ancient Egyptian recipes. The ancient Egyptian dishes that people prepare today are usually derived from hieroglyphic drawings of feasts, or knowledge of the crops grown and meats and fish consumed in the Nile region during ancient times.

An Ancient Egyptian Sweet

This recipe is an adaptation of what appears to have been a recipe on an ostracon, a broken piece of ancient pottery, dating back to 1600 BCE.

A SWEET TOOTH?

Sweetness was added to the ancient Egyptian diet in the form of honey, dates, figs, raisins and grapes. Dates are rich in protein as well as sugar.

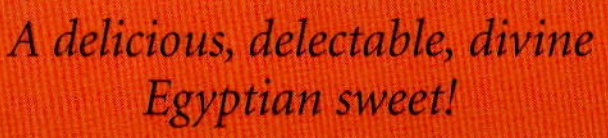

A delicious, delectable, divine Egyptian sweet!

Utensils

- a cup
- a fork
- a small bowl

Ingredients

- ½ cup of chopped dates
- 30 mL of warm water
- ½ teaspoon of cinnamon
- ¼ teaspoon of ground cardamom
- ¼ cup of finely chopped walnuts
- ½ cup warm, runny honey
- ½ cup of ground almonds (almond meal)
- 30 g of shredded coconut (optional)

some recipe ingredients

Method

Step 1

Place the chopped dates and warm water in a bowl. Soak the dates for five minutes.

Step 2

Use a fork to press the dates into a rough paste.

Step 3

Add the cinnamon and ground cardamom.

Step 4

Use the fork to mix in the cinnamon and ground cardamom.

Step 5

Add the chopped walnuts.

Step 6

Use the fork to mix the ingredients together.

Step 7

Form small ball shapes with the mixture.

Step 8

Roll each ball in the warm honey.

Step 9

Roll each ball in the almond meal and then in the shredded coconut (optional).

Step 10

Place the balls on a plate and cool in the fridge for 30 minutes.

7 Aswan High Dam, Egypt

The Nile basin suffers from varying levels of rainfall that cause periods of extreme floods and droughts. One solution the countries on the Nile have adopted is to build more storage facilities to help ease this problem. The Aswan High Dam was constructed during 1970–1971, to help regulate the flow of the waters in the Nile River and allow people to maximise the benefits of the vast amount of rainfall during summer.

THE DAM'S RESERVOIR

The Aswan High Dam's reservoir is Lake Nasser, which extends all the way across the Egyptian border into Sudan. It holds about 170 billion cubic metres of water.

Two **Aswan Dams**

1899–1902
The Aswan Low Dam was constructed.

1912
The dam was raised to cope with the rising water level in the dam's reservoir.

1933
The dam was further raised to mitigate the effects of flooding.

1970–1971
The Aswan High Dam was built about 6.5 kilometres from the Aswan Low Dam at a cost of one billion dollars.

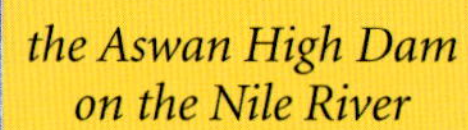
the Aswan High Dam on the Nile River

Positive Outcomes of the Aswan High Dam

1 Ability to Manage Water

The dam captures the summer rainfalls and allows people to better utilise the water where it is most needed.

2 Prevention of Flood Damage

The dam reduces the damaging effects of flooding in low-lying settlements along the river.

3 Ship and Boat Transportation

The regulated flow of the river makes it easier for water vessels to navigate.

4 Power Supply

The dam provides about half of Egypt's power requirements.

5 Irrigation for Crops

The water in the dam is used for irrigating the land to grow crops. Before the dam was built, only four per cent of Egypt's land was used for crops. With irrigation using the dam's reservoir, Lake Nasser, land use for crops has been increased to six per cent. Irrigation has helped to improve productivity during periods of low rainfall, and to prevent the effects of drought.

6 Fishing Industry

A thriving fishing industry has developed around Lake Nasser.

a fishing village on Lake Nasser, Aswan Egypt

EVAPORATION

As it is dry for much of the year, evaporation from the Nile River is another problem for the water resource management authorities.

Negative Outcomes of the Aswan High Dam

1 Decreased Fertility of the Land

Before the dam was constructed, summer floods used to carry nutrients from the Nile's riverbed to the floodplains – a natural process that farmers had relied on for centuries.

2 Increased Use of Chemically Made Fertilisers

Since the dam was built, farmers have had to buy chemically made fertilisers for their crops.

3 Reduced River Flow

The flow of the Nile has reduced and is no longer strong enough to prevent salt from the Mediterranean Sea entering the Nile's waters. This increases the salinity (salt content) of the soil around the river, which affects its quality.

4 Increased Cost of Crops

The cost of buying fertilisers has had an economic impact on the farmers – they may receive less profit for their crops.

5 Displacement of People

About 140 000 people of Egyptian and Sudanese origin had to move from their homes when the dam was constructed.

6 Disruption of Historical Sites

Many historic monuments and archaeological sites had to be excavated and relocated to other areas when the dam was built, which left much of the rich history of their origin flooded and lost forever.

The Temples of Abu Simbel

The Abu Simbel temples are two massive rock temples in southern Egypt. They were originally carved out of the mountainside during the reign of Pharaoh Ramses II in the thirteenth century BCE.

Dam Threatened Temples

The building of the Aswan High Dam threatened to flood the ancient temples, meaning the world would lose them forever. A decision was made to relocate the ancient structures onto an artificial hill, high above the water.

Between 1964 and 1968, the entire site was carefully cut into large stone blocks and reassembled in a new location. Archaeologists agree that this undertaking was one of the greatest feats of modern archaeological engineering. Today, thousands of tourists visit the 3200-year-old temples.

8 River Pollution

The unique ecosystem that is the Nile Basin is affected by many polluting factors. These include an increase in waste from a growing population and settlement construction, agricultural fertiliser run-off into the river and other waterways, industrial waste and the effects of an active tourism industry.

The future of the Nile, and of the millions of people who depend on it for their survival and livelihood, rests on the decisions about water management, sanitation and utilisation that all eleven countries that share the Nile Basin make.

a view from the Aswan High Dam of Lake Nasser

Before Dam Construction

Prior to the completion of the Aswan High Dam in 1971, the Nile's annual floodwaters flushed any pollutants away into the floodplains lining the river, as they flowed freely into the Mediterranean Sea.

After Dam Construction

Now, the Aswan High Dam and the smaller dams along the Nile trap the nutrient-rich floodwaters, and farmers have to add millions of tonnes of chemical fertilisers to the land. The chemical fertilisers run off from farm soil into the river, adding to the pollution that already exists from sewage (from settlements) and industrial waste from factories.

Finding Solutions

Agricultural scientists and biologists are endeavouring to find ways to improve the environmental conditions of the Nile's surrounding lakes, rivers, wetlands and irrigation and drainage canals. They aim to reduce the adverse effects of pollutants in order to improve water quality, and ultimately to protect the important fishing industry. One measure being discussed is to construct artificial wetlands that would trap pollutants from cities and prevent them from entering the Nile River and the Nile Delta. This would help prevent pollution from seeping into the soil and the Mediterranean Sea.

Water Pollution Leads to Diseases

Human sewage entering the rivers, dams, lakes and streams in the Nile Basin has led to a deterioration of water quality in many parts of the river, resulting in more waterborne diseases and disorders, such as diarrhoea and schistosomiasis.

Snail Fever

About 200 million people worldwide are infected with schistosomiasis, commonly known as "snail fever". It is a chronic disease that is spread through people coming into contact with water contaminated by sewage.

Freshwater snails in infested water carry the larvae of parasitic worms that can penetrate the skin of people who come into contact with the water by drinking or bathing in it. The worms live in blood vessels and can cause damage to the immune system and some organs. In children, long-term symptoms range from anaemia to a reduced ability to learn. The disease is also linked to cancer. In Africa, more than 200 000 people die each year from schistosomiasis.

a snail that can cause schistosomiasis

PREVENTION AVAILABLE

Safe and effective pills are available to prevent schistosomiasis, and if it is diagnosed and treated early, there is a high chance of recovery.

9 The Narrow Nile at Nubia

In the 1960s, the construction of the Aswan High Dam on the border of Egypt and Sudan forced the relocation of hundreds of thousands of Nubians.

Nubia is a region of Egypt and the Sudan. The Nile River is narrow and treacherous in much of Nubia due to several stretches of rapids and waterfalls called cataracts. Adding to the difficulties of boat travel here, as the river moves through northern Sudan, its course meanders, almost turning back the way it came for a stretch of about 250 kilometres. Boats attempting to travel upstream in this section not only need to move against the swift current, they also have to push against a strong north wind due to their change in direction.

Because of the difficulties of navigating the river here, in ancient times Nubia was quite isolated from the rest of the world. As a result, the cultures that sprang up in the region were distinct from those of ancient Egypt. One of the unique elements of Nubian culture is the beautiful mudbrick architecture of the houses, with their highly decorated thresholds and courtyards. When dams flooded many Nubian communities, villagers had to rebuild all of their houses on higher ground.

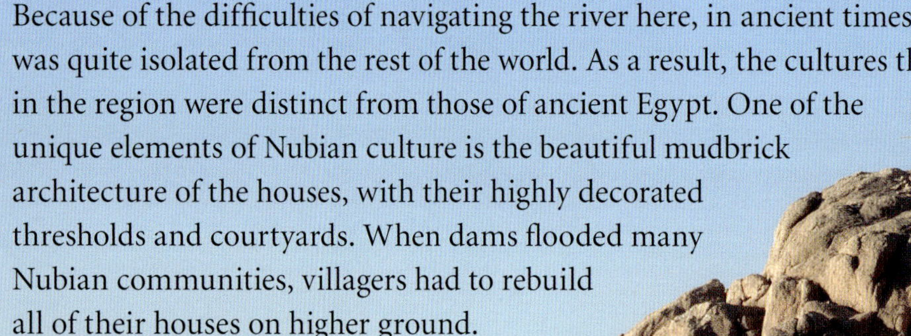

A Nubian woman selling spices in the marketplace of her home village.

Within the northern section between Aswan and Khartoum, in Nubia, the river passes through formations of hard igneous rock.

SCIENCE FEATURE

Climate Controls the River

No Rainfall

Rain does not fall in northern Nubia, so around that part of the Nile there is desert on either side.

Minimum Rainfall

In southern Nubia in Sudan, occasional summer rains enable grasses and some trees to grow.

Greater Rainfall

Further south, near Khartoum in Sudan, the heavier summer rains allow life to flourish in the soil as the landscape turns into large gum trees and acacia trees.

Two Main Seasons

In Egypt and northern Sudan, there are two main seasons. Typical years yield a long, cool winter from about November to March, and a long, hot summer from May to September, with a very short spring and autumn in between. There is very little rain at any time of the year. But upstream in southern Sudan and Ethiopia, summer comes with heavy downpours, which bring floods. The Nile swells to full capacity by the end of August in late summer. When the summer rains cease, the river levels gradually lower until the cycle is repeated the following summer.

Rainfalls from South to North

The Nile flows from the south to the north, and the climate varies greatly between the southern and northern countries.

Northern Nile Rainfall

The north of Egypt has less than 20 millimetres annual rainfall.

Southern Nile Rainfall

Southern Sudan receives about 750 millimetres of rainfall annually, while parts of Ethiopia can get up to 2000 millimetres of rain in a year.

10 Water Transportation and Tourism

The Felucca

The felucca is an ancient form of transportation that is still used to travel along the Nile River today. Traditionally, feluccas were wooden sailing boats, often with two sails. Although feluccas are not generally made of wood these days, their sails are still made of natural material, like cotton, and their layout remains unchanged. Some Egyptians still use feluccas for transport on the river, and many locals rent them out to tourists.

River Tours

As the world's longest river, brimming with a depth of ancient history, wildlife and a scenic river-based way of life that still exists today, the Nile draws many tourists in all forms of tour boats – from feluccas to mechanised barges to cruise ships. Feluccas are popular with tourists as a sustainable way to experience the Nile, propelled along by the gentle breezes and the river currents.

sailing on the Nile River at Aswan

Changes to River Flow Affect Tourism

Due to the falling water levels, in the area from Cairo to Luxor, luxury cruise ships were banned for 15 years. But in 2012 authorities lifted the ban, when water levels rose to acceptable levels once more.

Luxury cruises are popular on the Nile, with many going from Cairo, Egypt's capital, to Luxor.

WHITEWATER KAYAKING ON THE NILE

A whitewater kayaking company on the Murchison Falls in Uganda – where the water plunges at an extraordinary rate of 1600 cubic metres per second for about 70 metres – creates extreme thrills for whitewater enthusiasts!

TURN THE PAGE FOR DETAILS!

Kayak the Nile

Jamie Simpson is originally from Scotland and he is the owner of Kayak the Nile, Uganda.

In his own words, Jamie explains why he decided to start his kayak business on the Nile River and call this part of Uganda his home.

"I started Kayak the Nile in 1992 after working for various rafting companies. The Nile River is a really special river and I fell in love with it from Day 1. There is something very special about working on the source of the longest river in the world. The rapids are super-exciting and the wildlife is stunning. The people in Uganda are one of the best things. They must be the friendliest nation on Earth!"

arriving at the river's edge

Tourists absorb the breathtaking scenery before kayaking the Nile.

Jamie (left) reviews the kayaking conditions for the day.

Jamie (right) gets ready to join his tourist kayaker.

"This is how it's done, folks!"

some last-minute photographs and instructions before kayaking the Nile

Why Jamie Loves His Job

"What do I love about my job? Nothing is ever the same each day. Everybody I take on the river wants to be here and have the best day ever! It's hard not to be happy on such an amazing river. You cannot get bored with so many happy people around. It's my passion to show people the river that I like to call home and the amazing wildlife.

"Another big plus is training local villagers with skills that they would not normally have a chance to learn. We now have over 20 Ugandan Raft Guides and kayakers of a world-class standard earning a great living from the sport. Some of them have been travelling overseas and we even have a Ugandan kayaking team that competes in the World Championships each year."

The Nile's Animal Life

Jamie quickly took this snap of a crocodile!

Birdlife is abundant along the river banks.

11 The Nile Swimmers Project

Sudanese villagers participating in lifesaving training

The sun sets on the Nile River in Sudan.

From the Founder ...

Tom Mecrow is a lifesaving training instructor with the Royal Life Saving Society, UK. He explains, "Nile Swimmers is a unique drowning-prevention project based on the River Nile in Africa. We teach people how to swim, and give them lifesaving skills so that they can rescue themselves and others in difficulty. We work with local organisations, including the Sudanese Sea Scouts. Drowning is a leading cause of death for people living near the Nile. People use the river for many activities including washing, bathing, swimming and transportation."

Emmanuel, a refugee from Uganda living in Sudan, is now a Nile Swimmers Project instructor.

Emmanuel demonstrates how to position the body before commencing resuscitation.

Africa has a high rate of death from drowning, and the treacherous parts of the Nile River are an ever-present danger for those who live on its banks.

The Nile Swimmers Project was set up by Tom Mecrow and Dan Graham to share swimming and lifesaving skills in Sudan, and to facilitate discussion about water safety ideas for communities. Those who take part in the Project's training sessions take these skills and the water safety ideas generated in the discussions back to their villages and communities in Sudan and along the Nile.

a section of rapids on the White Nile, Uganda

Emmanuel demonstrates CPR (cardiopulmonary resuscitation) for Sudanese villagers.

Index

Glossary

climate zone An area having a particular climate

ecosystem A network of plants and animals all depending on each other in their natural environment

evaporation The process by which liquid becomes a vapour, as when heat from the Sun causes river water to vaporise and be lost

fertile Able to support abundant crops and other vegetation

flood plains A flat plain beside a river that is regularly flooded when the water is high

irrigation The creation of artificial channels to draw water from a river into the surrounding land

monsoonal Relating to an annual period of heavy rain, or monsoon

pollutant A substance that enters the environment and damages it

sustainable Able to be continued without hurting the environment or running out of natural resources

tributaries Streams that flow into a larger stream